Fireweed in
the spring

Fireweed

Violets in the spring

A field of Fireweed in summer

Fireweed flower

Fireweed in seed

Fireweed in fall

A field of fireweed in the fall

Linnaea borealis (Twinflower)

LINNAEA'S WORLD

By

Verna E. Pratt

Illustrated by

Allene Franklin

Alaskakrafts, Inc.
Post Office Box 210087
Anchorage, AK 99521-0087

First Printing

Library of Congress Catalog Card Number.......96-83135

ISBN 0-9623192-5-2

Printed in Hong Kong through
DNP (AMERICA), Inc.

Author-------Verna E. Pratt

Line drawings-------Verna E. Pratt

Illustrator-------Allene Franklin

Editor-------Frank G. Pratt

All photographs are by Verna and Frank Pratt unless otherwise noted.

<u>Dedication</u>

This volume is dedicated to our granddaughter, Angelina, who inspired us to produce this book, and to all the future botanists and artists of the world. It is our hope that this book will inspire and aid them in their search for happiness and fulfillment in life through art and nature.

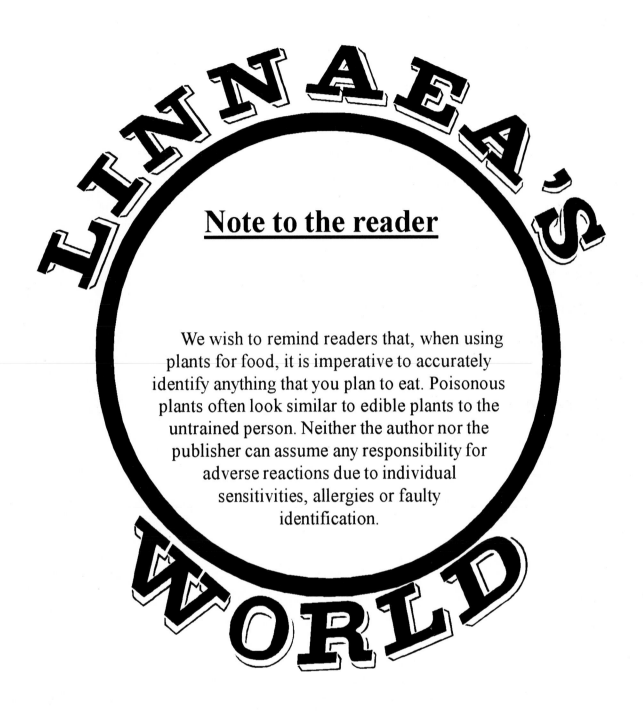

LINNAEA'S WORLD

Note to the reader

We wish to remind readers that, when using plants for food, it is imperative to accurately identify anything that you plan to eat. Poisonous plants often look similar to edible plants to the untrained person. Neither the author nor the publisher can assume any responsibility for adverse reactions due to individual sensitivities, allergies or faulty identification.

The forest flower

Linnaea
is only 4 years old and
very small and dainty for her age.

She lives in a log house in the
forest with her mother and father.
No other people live close by. Their
friends are the plants, animals, and
birds of the forest.

Many years ago, her father came
to Alaska to live in the wilderness, far
away from the big cities. He built their
home from the very large trees that
he cut down.

He removed all of the branches
and peeled off the bark to make
them into smooth logs,
and then placed them
close together
to keep out
the cold
winter
winds.

She enjoys sitting
on the rocky
knoll overlooking
the clearing where
trees once grew. It is warm and
sunny in the meadow and many
flowers bloom there in the summer.
Colorful butterflies flutter from flower to
flower tasting the sweet nectar. If she stands
really still she can see the colorful spots
and patterns on their wings. Once she tried
to catch one, but it moved too quickly. "It
was best," her mother said, "you might rub
the powder off their wings, and then they
could not fly. They must be able to fly from
flower to flower and gather the nectar as
that is their food.

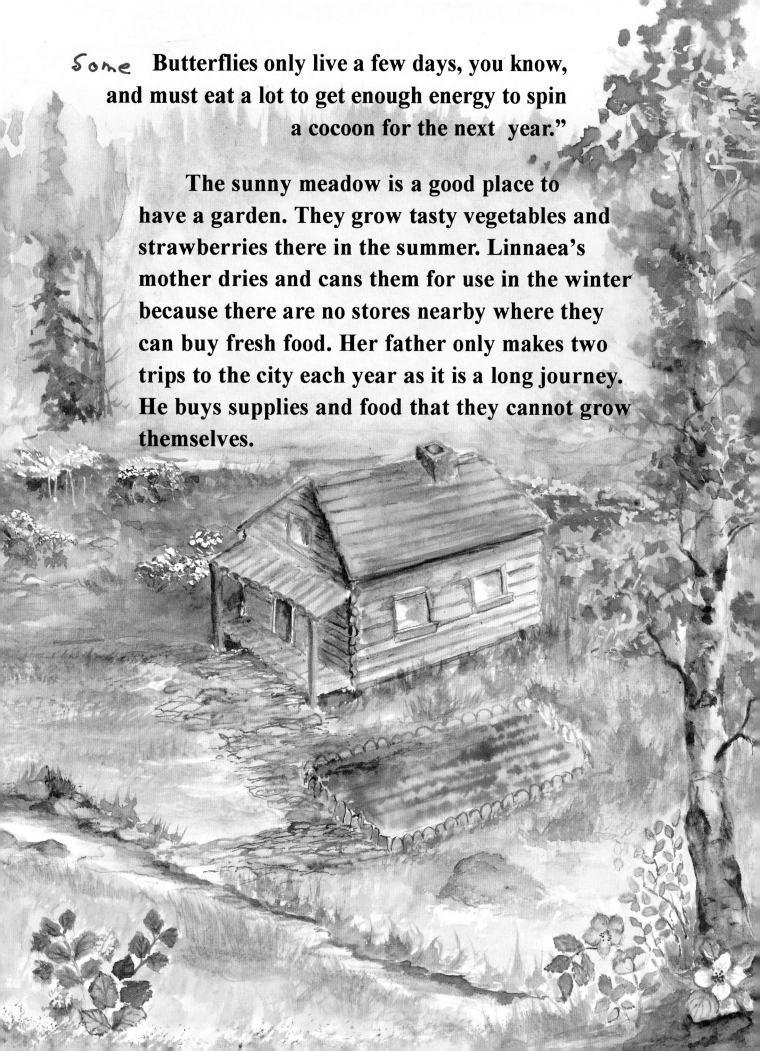

Some Butterflies only live a few days, you know,
and must eat a lot to get enough energy to spin
a cocoon for the next year."

The sunny meadow is a good place to
have a garden. They grow tasty vegetables and
strawberries there in the summer. Linnaea's
mother dries and cans them for use in the winter
because there are no stores nearby where they
can buy fresh food. Her father only makes two
trips to the city each year as it is a long journey.
He buys supplies and food that they cannot grow
themselves.

It is August now and time to pick berries. They will all go deep into the forest near a stream to pick blueberries. The bushes are very tall so Linnaea can only reach the lowest branches. Someday she will be big enough to pick all of the berries.

Bears also like the berries, so her father always goes with them. He carries a rifle to scare the bears away if they happen to come too close. There are plenty of berries for everyone so they always leave some for the bears and birds.

Her father told her that bears need to eat all of the time in the summer to make them fat. During the winter they like to sleep most of the time, living off of the fat stored in their bodies.

Linnaea has never seen a bear. Her father says that they usually stay in the forest and run away when they hear people coming. Her mother will make tasty jellies and pies from the blueberries that they pick. Linnaea likes the blueberry syrup for her pancakes best of all.

She likes these trips into the forest. There are so many different things to see.

She is never allowed to go there alone.

Fall is coming and the fireweed has gone to seed.

The bright red rose hips are ready to pick and dry. Her mother grinds or chops them and uses them in place of nuts in cookies and breads. Linnaea does not like to pick these because the bushes have prickles on them that stick into her fingers and arms.

Their brightly colored leaves and the leaves and berries of the Bunchberry plants make a colorful border at the edge of the forest. Linnaea likes this time of year. It looks like someone splashed bright paint on the bushes and trees.

Her mother does not pick the Bunchberries that cover the ground under the trees. Some people say that you might feel sick if you eat too many of them, but small animals sample them and carry them to their cache (*) to eat in the winter.

*A cache is a place to store food. It might be in or under a log or in a tunnel in the ground.

All of the small animals will need a lot of food to keep them warm during the long, cold winter. They will only go out if they need more food than they collected during the summer.

Linnaea wonders what it must be like to be a little mouse? How can they find their way through all the tall grass and plants. There are so many trails. It seems like they might get lost.

Her father said that she would surely get lost if she went into the forest.

There are so many trails there that the animals use and they cross each other going in all directions.

It must be very exciting there.

Some day, when she is old enough, she would like to go into the forest alone.

Linnaea likes to play just inside the edge of the forest. It seems like a giant fairyland. It is very different from the meadow and the sunny hillside. Many different plants grow there. They might not be able to live out in the bright sunshine.

It is cool and moist under the big trees.

Only a little sun can reach down through the branches.

There are many different mushrooms growing in the moss.

Sometimes
she imagines that she is a tiny, tiny
fairy holding a parasol mushroom. She
is much too big to get under it, so she holds
it up to see the light shine through the thin
flesh. It looks just like a tiny umbrella. Linnaea
has only seen umbrellas in her picture books.
Her mother says that people in the cities hold
them over their heads to keep their clothes
dry when they go outside on rainy days.

The large rounded Bolete mushrooms
look like soft spongy foot stools. She can
see where the small animals have been
taking bites out of them.

The Cranberries are ripe now and while Linnaea and
her mother pick the berries, her father will go to
the city for their winter supplies.
It is a long journey to the city, so he will go alone.
His big backpack looks empty now,
but it will be full when he returns.
He must travel through the forest and then
take their canoe across a very long lake.
From there he walks over the hills to the city.
"Someday," he says, "you will be strong
enough to go too,
Linnaea."

She is always excited
when he returns.

He always brings back something
new. She remembers how tasty the
oranges were last
spring and how
much fun she had
playing with
the colorful
kite.

The berries are picked,
and her mother is busy making jelly.
While Linnaea
waits for her father to return
from the city, she goes up on the hill and watches all the
large birds preparing to fly south, and the small animals
gathering
food.

The bright-colored leaves of fireweed fill the meadow and the fluffy seeds float through the air. Some fly over to the edge of the forest where the bright colored trees and shrubs are growing.

This is Linnaea's world. A home in the forest.

It was only a few days since her father went away, but it seemed like such a long, long time. Linnaea was anxious and curious to see what exciting new things he might bring back. He said there were so many different things in the city. So much to wonder about when you have never been there.

She wonders what it must be like
on the other side of the trees,
and across the lake.

Her father said there are big mountains there and
fast-moving rivers. He said she was much too
small to travel such a long distance. Someday
she would see the city with all its big houses
so close together. He said that people ride
around in cars
and buses.

One time he brought back a book
about people living in the city. It was
hard for Linnaea to imagine such a
place with so many
people and so few
plants and trees
and no place
to play.

There are no wild animals there because the forests are all gone.

Only houses are there now. People have tame animals living in their homes. They call them "pets". What a strange world this seems to Linnaea. She has never seen a dog, but thinks that she would like to have one to play with.

Her father said, "A dog might frighten the wild animals away. Perhaps, someday a kitten would be better, as it probably would not frighten the other animals.

Perhaps next Spring."

How excited she was when her father returned with big, sweet, juicy red apples.

"Where do they get the apples," said Linnaea.

"They grow on trees," he said.

"We should plant an apple tree in the meadow," she said.

"We will see," he said, "but I believe it is too cold here in the north country. Now I must go back to the lake to get more supplies from the canoe. There was too much for me to carry in one trip." This time he brought back ham, which he said was meat from a pig. He said pigs once were wild like moose and bears, but now people raise them in fenced areas and sell them for food.

Soon her father will go out in the forest and hunt wild animals for food before the snow comes and walking becomes difficult. He will make sure to only look for animals that do not have babies to care for.

That night her mother read her a new book on
farm animals. Some day she would see
these animals and where they
live in pens and cages.

Her father played his fiddle
while she looked at the
pictures in the book.

Suddenly, the days are colder and today is dark and cloudy. The air feels different. A strong breeze is blowing the leaves off the trees and shrubs.

Small birds are hopping along the ground gathering seeds. Chickadees fly back and forth gathering seeds from the tall Cow Parsnip plants. Pieces of shell are under the trees where the birds sit and eat the soft nut meat inside.

The small birds seem to know that snow is coming as they rush around for food.

They will need a lot of food to keep them warm as the nights get colder.

Her father is busy
cutting wood for their stove and fireplace.

They will need a lot of wood
to keep them warm during the winter.

Slowly snow starts falling to
the ground. The first snowfall
always excites Linnaea.

The flakes are so large
and look like lace
when they land
on her jacket.

Everyone is preparing for winter now.
Soon the ground will be covered with a
blanket of white. The small plants will
rest until the weather warms up and
spring comes again.

Linnaea was really surprised in the morning
when she looked out the window.

She discovered that winter had come,
quickly and softly during the night
while they were all asleep.

The branches of the spruce trees
were heavy with snow and provided
a warm place for birds and small
animals to hide.

Her father told her that the bears
would find a dry cave to sleep in
during the winter and the small
animals will spend much of
the time in their homes
beneath the ground.

Moose and deer wander around
eating branches of trees and
shrubs. They will find a warm
place between the trees and bed
down in the snow.

Linnaea wondered how they could keep warm, but her
father said the snow was like a blanket to them
and their hair was like a fur coat.

When she went outdoors to play she saw footprints in the snow. They went from shrub to shrub, and the branches were freshly chewed. Under a Highbush Cranberry shrub, she saw a Snowshoe Hare.

He was hiding, but she saw him anyway. He still had some of his summer colors and the brown hairs were easy to see against the fresh white snow. Soon he will be all white and harder to see. In the spring the new brown hairs will grow again, and he will easily hide in the shrubs and grass again.

She wanted to touch him, to see how soft his hair was but he quickly hopped away. She thought that she would like to have a hare for a pet, but her father said, "No, Linnaea, a hare would not stay unless you put him in a cage. It would be wrong to do that to a wild animal. It would be frightened and they keep warm by hopping around and finding food."

"No! That would not be right."

Linnaea spends much of her time indoors in the winter because the days are dark and cold.

It is warm and cozy inside and the crackling of the wood burning in the fireplace is a pleasant and familiar sound.

She spends many hours lying on the rug looking at the books her father brought her.

She would really like to see all the animals on the farms, but life outside the forest and city life seem so strange to her.

Linnaea said, "Why do they call this animal that looks like a Snowshoe Hare a rabbit?"

"They really are very much alike." said her father, "A Rabbit is born without any hair on its body, so he must be kept warm by his mother. A Hare is born with hair."

Today is Thanksgiving Day, and the family will
have a nice meal of Spruce Hen and cranberry
sauce made from the berries they picked in
the fall. Linnaea's mother told her that most
people in the city have turkey or goose to eat.
Linnaea had only seen these birds in a book.
She could not imagine how large they must be.
How could a bird that large fly? Her mother also
said, "People in the city will have pumpkin pie.
It tastes very much like our rose-hip pie.
Perhaps we will try to grow a
pumpkin next year."

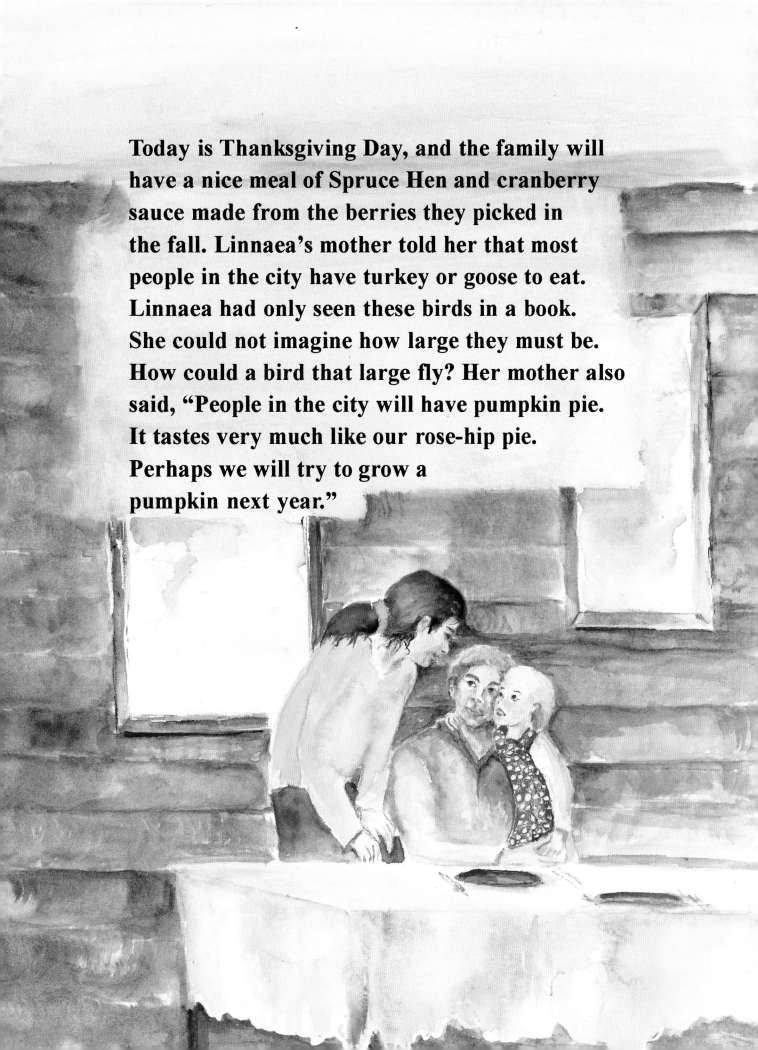

As soon as there was light in the sky, Linnaea's father walked off through the forest. She wonders how he can walk so well on snowshoes. She tried once but they were so big and heavy that she could not lift her feet off the ground.

Today, he will fish at the lake. She has never watched him catch fish. Someday when she is bigger and can walk that far she will go with him.

The ice on the lake is frozen, so he needs to cut a hole in the ice before fishing.

It was almost dark when he returned with the fish he had caught.

The nights are clear and very dark now and sometimes the Northern Lights dance across the sky, lighting up the snow below.

"People in the city seldom see these lights," her father says, "because they have so many other lights around them." "You see, Linnaea," he said, "wherever a person lives, there is something special to enjoy. Something that other people cannot have or do. We have bright lights in the sky. In the city they have lights on streets and in the buildings."

As the days grow longer, the snow melts quickly from the rocky knoll.

The buds on the willows and aspen trees are soft and fluffy and covered with bees.

Small insects are starting to crawl around finding food and new life after a long winter rest.

Soon the currants will be blooming and the bright red buds on the Highbush Cranberries will become leaves.

SPRING is here.

Linnaea pulled a few branches from the willow shrub and ran down the hill to show her mother the first flowers of spring.

"Most people call them catkins or Pussy Willows," her mother said, "because they feel like the soft hair of a kitten."

"Oh, I wish I had a kitten to play with," said Linnaea.

"But all of the animals in the forest are your friends," her father replied.

"Yes," she said, "but they don't stay and play with me. Someday, I would like a soft, fuzzy animal that does not run away from me."

Linnaea likes this time of year because there are so many new plants coming up through the ground. So many tasty new young plants to pick and eat. The bright red shoots of fireweed are coming up all over the meadow, and soon the violets and ferns will appear down near the stream. It has been a long while since they have had tasty fresh salads to eat. The whole family really enjoys the tasty, tightly curled up leaves of the ferns. Her mother calls them fiddleheads because they look like the neck of the fiddle that Linnaea's father plays.

New plants seem to appear every day and they grow very fast as the days grow warm and the sun stays out longer. Soon it will be light most of the day.

Her father is busy preparing the garden in the middle of the meadow. As soon as the ground is ready, he will go to the city again.

The ice should be melted from the lake now and seeds for the garden are needed. He said that he would bring back pumpkin seeds to grow. Linnaea has never seen a pumpkin and wonders what else he might bring back.

A small bee flew into a blueberry flower and bounced back and forth trying to get out.

Her father said the flowers taste good so she tried some. They were sweet like the candy her mother sometimes makes. No wonder the bees like the nectar so much.

It was an exciting day when her father returned. He brought back seeds that they will plant --- even pumpkin seeds.

He also brought a small tree that they will plant in the meadow. The man in the store said that a Crabapple tree would be best for them to grow because most apple trees need warmer weather. Crabapples are small sour apples, but they make very good jelly, juice and applesauce. It will take a long while to grow, but it was the largest tree that her father could carry back through the forest.

Perhaps next year it will have some flowers and apples on it.

Linnaea's father told her to look inside his pack, and this was the best surprise of all.

A small fluffy striped kitten with white paws.

"Oh," said Linnaea, "I think I will call her Pussy Willow, or maybe Socks, or maybe Tiger."

"Let's think about it for a while," said her mother. "We want to choose the right name for her."

For the next few days, Linnaea watched her playful kitten run through the grass, and chase the flies and bees. She seemed to play with everything she saw. Once she made a bee angry and he stung her on her nose.

"I will call her 'Tiger'", Linnaea said.

"Perhaps, we should call her Trouble," her father said and laughed as the kitten leaped high into the air.

Linnaea thinks that the Low-bush Cranberry flowers look like fairy's petticoats. But imagine how large they must seem to the tiny insect crawling around inside. Her kitten grabbed at the insect and ate the flower.

"Was it okay," she asked her father, "for Tiger to eat the flower?"

"Yes," he replied, "but someday she might eat the wrong thing. She is very foolish. I really think we should name her Trouble. She has been digging in the garden, you know and chasing birds and mice, too. Perhaps I should not have brought her home."

"I'll watch her," said Linnaea, "I'll teach Tiger not to do bad things. I really will watch her. She'll be no trouble at all."

In the days that followed, Tiger (or Trouble as she was usually called), got into mischief wherever she went. She followed Linnaea everywhere.

Flowers were everywhere now. Large pink Roses and white Dogwood flowers on the edge of the forest. Single Delights growing on the moss-covered logs. Her mother said that some people called it Shy Maiden because it always hangs its head and faces the ground like a bashful child.

It is such a pretty flower. Some of the seed pods from last years flowers are still there like little lanterns on a post.

My, how much to see when you are close to the ground.

Linnaea has seen so many changes this past year. Surely, by now, she is big enough to make the long journey to the city with her father.

"No," her father says, "not quite yet. First you must be able to make the long trip through the forest to the lake and back. That is far enough for the first time. Walking through the forest is not easy. There are steep hills to climb, large fallen trees to climb over, and a stream to cross. Perhaps in the spring. No, not yet, Linnaea!"

One day while lying on the moss on the edge of the
forest, Linnaea looked up at an old stump covered with small
pink and whte flowers. They were like small bells hanging on
a thin stem.

They smelled so nice when she was close to them.
It was such a friendly plant — never crowding
or pushing others around. The small
leaves are evergreen, so can be
seen even in the winter. They
are on long runners that
go under and around
the other plants.

"Mother,"
Linnaea said,
"Come and see
my favorite
plant."

"Oh, how nice," her mother said, "that you should choose this plant. The plant you like is called Twinflower because it has two flowers on each stem. Perhaps I should tell you a story now."

"Many years ago, before you were born, I met some people in the forest. They were there for many days. They were scientists and were studying the plants that grow here. Each time I met them they would help me learn some more plant names. We talked a lot about Twinflower as that is also my favorite plant. They explained to me that it only grows in cooler northern areas, but that it is found in many countries.

They said that it was also the favorite plant of a famous scientist from Sweden many, many years ago. His full name was Carolus Linnaeus, but we will call him Carl. Twinflower also grows in Sweden. Most people know plants by their common names and in different places they call them by different names. Carl decided that each plant should have one name, a scientific name, to be used all over the world. Scientists still use the names that he gave to plants. He is called the father of botany, which is the study of plants.

He gave Twinflower his name and called it Linnaea borealis. Borealis means north and Twinflower grows only in cool northern areas. They also told me that Linnaea is a common name for girls in Sweden."

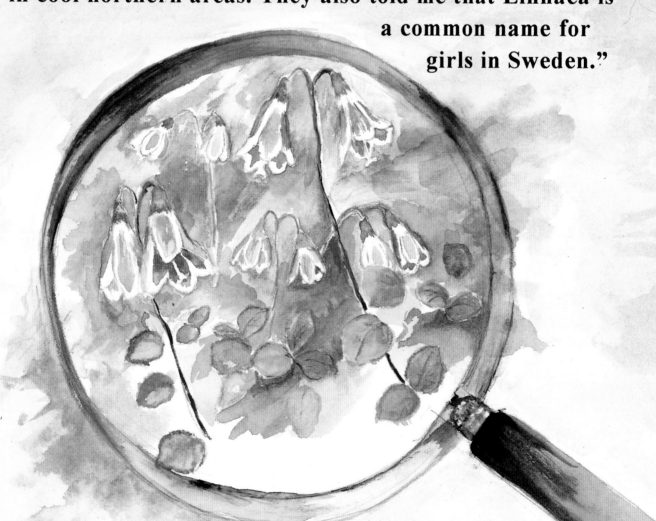

"You were such a tiny and delicate baby, when you were born, that we decided to name you Linnaea after Twinflower, the delicate sweet flower of our forest. Perhaps this is why you are so attracted to this fairyland flower that carpets the forest floor.

You and the Twinflower are twin flowers of the forest.

You are our Linnaea of the forest."

This is your world, Linnaea!

Pictorial Glossary

Cache—A place to store food high above the ground, out of the reach of animals. A ladder is used for people to reach the food.

Cocoon—A soft case or covering around an insect in the young stage to protect it from damage and too much rain. Something like a soft shell on an egg.

Evergreen—Leaves that stay green all year and do not fall off of the plant, shrub (bush), or tree in the winter. Usually they are thick or leathery. Most evergreen leaves are on trees or shrubs.

Hip—Fruit of a rose flower. Very much like a small dry apple.

Knoll—A small hill.

Nectar—A sweet juice, like honey, that attracts insects to a flower to pollinate it so that it will produce seeds. Often it is sticky and sometimes it smells good, too. Sometimes flowers have stripes on their petals to lead the insects to the nectar and pollen.

Plants—Plants are living things with roots that attach them to the ground and absorb water and food. Usually, when people mention plants they are referring to the ones with soft stems that die down to the ground in the winter. Shrubs (bushes) and trees have tough woody stems that stay alive above the ground during the winter. Trees usually have one main trunk, arising out of the ground, shrubs usually have many.

Plant

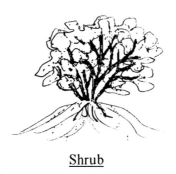
Shrub

Tree

Pictorial Glossary

Prickles—Sharp, pointed, needle-like growths on the stems of some shrubs. They are attached to only the outer skin of the plant. Thorns grow deeper into the stems. Thorns and prickles are on plants to discourage animals from eating them. Many plants also have hairs on their stems or leaves. Most hairs deflect the sun so that the plants don't get sunburned, or trap moisture to water the plants. Some hairs, however, send out irritating acids that make your skin itch or cause a rash. Cow Parsnip has this type of hairs and can be very irritating to some people.

Snow Shoes—Large, flat objects that people wear strapped to their boots when they go out in deep snow. This allows them to walk on top of the snow.

Spruce Hen—A wild bird that looks something like a chicken with very short legs.

Author / Photographer

Verna E. Pratt

Raised on the family farm in the small town of West Newbury, Massachusetts. After raising her family, she found herself as an individual in arts, crafts, photography, and writing. She was the primary activist in forming the Alaska Native Plant Society in 1982. She enjoys helping others learn about wildflowers by leading field trips, giving lectures and teaching wildflower identification classes.

She is a member of:

Alaska Master Gardeners Association
Wildflower Garden Club
Arts and Crafts League of Alaska
Alaska Orchid Society
North American Orchid Alliance
North American Rock Garden Society
New England Wildflower Society

Frank G. Pratt

Born in Cambridge, Massachusetts. Moved to West Newbury, Mass. as a high school student; and, while serving as an Army officer, was transferred to Alaska in 1966.

A pharmacist by profession, he had a natural interest in plants. His real interest in wildflower photography developed; however, when it became clear that this was one way for he and Verna to spend more time together with common interests. It was the old adage of, "If you can't beat 'em, join 'em".

When asked about his interest in wildflower photography, he often replies that Verna has made a poor hunter out of him, as he now hikes looking at the ground rather than the horizon.

He is a member of:

Alaska Pharmaceutical Association
American Radio Relay League
Anchorage Amateur Radio Club
National Rifle Association
Quarter Century Wireless Association
Radio Amateur Satellite Association

Both are members of the Alaska Native Plant Society (ANPS), Alaska Society of Outdoor and Nature Photographers (ASONP), North American Nature Photographers Association (NANPA), American Society of Media Photographers (ASMP), and the National Press Photographers Association (NPPA). They spend much of their time in the summer camping, hiking, exploring and photographing Alaska, especially the wildflowers.

The Artist

Allene Franklin

Photo by Wendy DiCaprio

Born in Fort Worth, Texas, and drove up the ALCAN Highway with her family in 1951 to make Anchorage, Alaska, her home.

She has had a life long interest in art and music and is an accomplished musician on piano and accordion. Her natural artistic talents have been enhanced by attending workshops of several nationally recognized artists, and from art courses at the University of Alaska, Anchorage. In 1979, she won 1st prize for an oil portrait in the Alaska Centennial art competition.

In addition to her commissioned work, Allene has exhibited in art galleries in Anchorage and Juneau. She is a member of the Alaska Artists' Guild, The Alaska Watercolor Society, and an associate member of the Northwest Watercolor Society.

She is an accomplished photographer who enjoys working out-of-doors, so most of her work is done from field sketches and photographs taken on location. She works in oils, acrylics, watercolors and pastels; and, works mainly on Alaska landscapes, wildlife, and birds.

About her art, Allene says: *"We are truly alone and yet art transcends that separateness. It is my privilege and pleasure to share the gift of being alive through painting. If I can communicate with another person through painting, I will be delighted. If I can cause him to communicate with himself, I will have achieved success."*

The Publisher

Alaskakrafts, Inc.
P. O. Box 210087
Anchorage, AK 99521-0087

Book publishing began in 1987 when the question, "What are we going to do with all of these slides?", came up. Add to this the vital need for an easy to use Alaska Wildflower book, computers with fabulous capabilities, a lot of time and love of what you are doing and the following books are now available:

Field Guide to Alaskan Wildflowers—a guide to the most common plants in Southcentral and Interior Alaska in areas accessible by road. ---------------------------- $15.95

Wildflowers along the Alaska Highway—a complete guide to all plants observed from Dawson Creek, British Columbia to Fairbanks, Alaska. -------------------- $19.95

Wildflowers of Denali National Park—a complete guide to all plants seen at the time of printing. --- $16.95

Alaska's Wild Berries and Berry-like fruit—a guide to all the berries in Alaska from Ketchikan to the North Slope. --------------------------------------- $9.95

Fiddle head fern
(new spring growth)

Cow Parsnip

Cow Parsnip seeds

Rose flower

Ferns in the summer

Blueberry flowers

Blueberries

Rose hip (fruit of Rose flower)